BIG SISTERS are BAD WITCHES

by MORSE HAMILTON pictures by MARYLIN HAFNER

Greenwillow Books, New York

Library of Congress Cataloging in Publication Data
Hamilton, Morse.   Big sisters are bad witches.
Summary: The sibling rivalry of two sisters
improves when a third child on the way promises
to turn little sister into big sister.
[1. Sibling rivalry—Fiction.   2. Brothers
and sisters—Fiction.   3. Babies—Fiction]
I. Hafner, Marylin.   II. Title.   PZ7.H18265Bi
[E]   79-24907   ISBN 0-688-80268-0
ISBN 0-688-84268-2 lib. bdg.

For
Jennifer
—Morse Hamilton

For Katherine
and Sylvia
—Marylin Hafner

I want a baby brother. His name will be Kate, just like me. He will have brown hair and brown eyes like me. I will let him have a piece of gum from my pack whenever he wants. I will let him play with my dolls whenever he wants to.

I will never say, "You're bothering me, Kate!"
to him. If I'm watching television, he can sit
next to me in the red chair. I will put my arm
around him. He can even suck his thumb
if he wants to.
"You know what, Kate?" he will say.
"What, Kate?" I will say.
"Big sisters are bad witches."
"Yeah," I will say. "They sure are."

I was bad, but so was my big sister Emily.
Mrs. Wetherbee said she had never seen such a bad
girl. She must have meant Emily, because Emily's the
one who started it. She was playing with my father's
typewriter, and she isn't supposed to.

"Hi, Em," I said—like that—in a nice voice.
"Can I type, too?"
"Kate! You're ruining my report!"
When I climbed on the desk to watch, she
pushed me, and I accidentally knocked my
father's giraffe off and it broke.

"Look what you've done!" Emily shouted, pulling at my sweater. She almost ripped it and tore one of the buttons off, and it's my father's favorite sweater. He says I look very pretty in it.
I told her my father was going to be mad when he found out that she had been playing with his typewriter. "My daddy is very nice," I said. "You shouldn't have broken his giraffe, you bad girl."
Then she hit me—hard—on the arm. It hurt.
I started to cry because it hurt so much.
"Oh, crybaby. I only touched you," Emily said.

I ran downstairs where Mrs. Wetherbee was watching television.

"What's this? What's this?" she said, letting me get on her lap.

Emily shouted from the top of the stairs, "She's being terrible. She keeps bothering me, and I can't get my report done. And she broke my father's giraffe."

I hugged Mrs. Wetherbee as hard as I could and put my face against her front and cried some more.

"Kate," she said. "Kate, Kate, Kate."

Now I'm waiting for my father to get home.
Emily is watching television and she won't let me
sit by her. I said I was sorry. When my father gets
home, I'm going to run and meet him and give
him the biggest hug and kiss in the whole world.
But he will probably spank me anyway, because
I've been bad.
But Emily was bad, too. And if my father spanks
me, he will be bad, too.
Everyone's bad in this house except my mother
and my spider, Jennifer.

A little black spider lives behind my dresser.
I saw it when I climbed back there to get my
sock. My mother hates spiders, but my father
and I don't. I told Emily about it.
"Oh, neat, Kate. What's its name?"
"Jennifer."
I named it Jennifer after Em's best friend, because
she's small, too. Jennifer doesn't like to play with
me, because she says I'm small.

Jennifer went as a pickle for Halloween. I tried to get her to go as a spider, but she said that was stupid.

I will go and see what the spider is doing, and then I will come right back.

The spider's just sitting there, all alone. Just thinking.

My father is a tough hombre. I'm my father's
partner.
"Put it there, partner," he said when he came
 home.
"Put it there, partner," I said.
"Aren't you going to spank her?" Emily said.

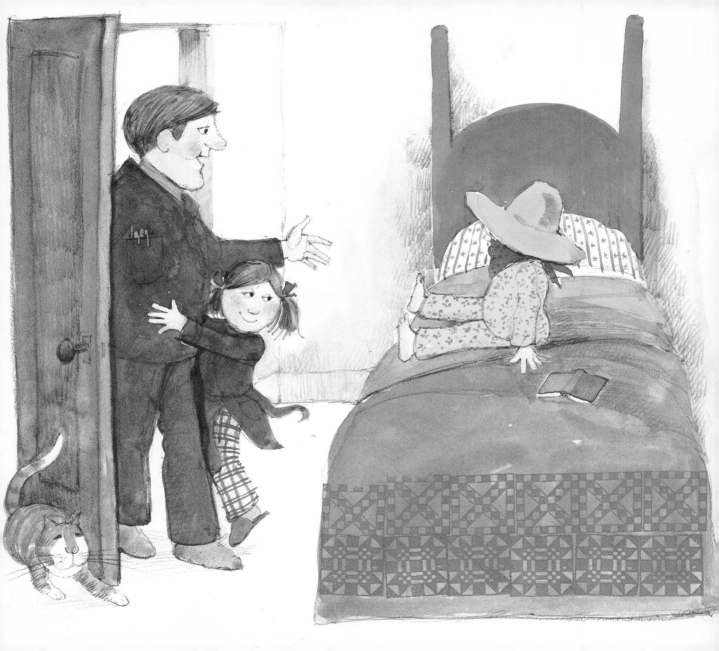

We all sat in the red chair, and my father hugged
me and my sister. It was very crowded.
"Now I want you to listen to me," he said. "I have
something to tell you."
"Mom had a baby brother called Kate," I said.
"Not another Kate!" Emily said, but she didn't
mean it in a bad way, because she started
laughing.
We all laughed.

"We have a Kate," my father said. "But you're right. The new baby is a boy. Now Kate will know what it's like to be a little sister and a big sister."

Emily was in a very good mood tonight.
We played with all our dolls and she
taught me a new song and she read
me a story.
Emily's not really a bad witch.
"Can I have a stick of gum from your
pack, Em?"

THE END